Dunc
and the
Greased Sticks
of Doom

Gary Paulsen

Dunc and the Greased Sticks of Doom

A YEARLING BOOK

Published by
Dell Publishing
a division of
Bantam Doubleday Dell Publishing Group, Inc.
1540 Broadway
New York, New York 10036

The trademark Yearling® is registered in the U.S. Patent and Trademark Office.

The trademark Dell® is registered in the U.S. Patent and Trademark Office.

ISBN: 0-440-40940-3

Printed in the United States of America

November 1994

10 9 8 7 6 5 4 3 2 1

OPM

Dunc
and the
Greased Sticks
of Doom

Chapter · 1

The phone rang.

Amos moved.

He was sitting on the couch watching television—a show about how much people could lift when they were scared—and he was in motion before the first ring was half over. He knew it was Melissa Hansen calling him. He could tell by the certain insistent pulse of the ring. Amos Binder was in love with Melissa Hansen and would marry her someday—even though she had never so much as acknowledged his presence on the planet, let alone called him. He had to get that phone.

1

Unfortunately, he forgot about the bowl of popcorn in his lap. Nor did he hear his mother's scream. He didn't feel Scruff grab his ankle and pull, and to make matters worse, the dog's tripping him increased his air speed and hang time. Amos was completely airborne all the way into the kitchen.

He knew he wouldn't make it when he hit the chair. Amos ricocheted and flew across the kitchen table where dinner had been set, sending the plate of steaks flying toward a grateful Scruff.

Amos lay motionless on the floor. His sister, Amy, who cared for the dog way more than she did for him, grabbed the phone and answered it.

"Hello?"

She listened for a moment, then handed Amos the phone with a look of disgust and stepped over him as if he were road kill.

"Amos, did you try for the phone again?" It was Dunc, his best friend for life.

"Naw, I just dropped the phone. What's going on?" Amos tossed the steak on his chest to Scruff and stood up.

"What do you know about skiing?"

"Only that you strap two waxed sticks to your feet and let gravity drag you down a hill at a deadly speed. Why?" Amos wiped meat juice off his forehead.

"My parents and I are going skiing over Christmas vacation. They said you could come if you wanted to go."

"Dunc, I know we're friends. But the trouble you always get me into would be disastrous on the ski slopes. Besides, I have to go to my grandparents' house on Christmas."

"Think about what you're saying, Amos. You'd rather go eat peanut brittle and have your cheeks pinched than bomb down the slopes of a mountain at death-defying speeds? At least ask, you never know. They might say yes."

Amos hoped his parents would say no. That way he wouldn't have to lose honor with Dunc. So he asked as nonchalantly as possible. When his parents didn't hesitate, he knew he was in trouble.

They said yes as though he were asking to go to the mall. Didn't they realize he

3

would probably end up a smudge on a mountain?

There was silence on the phone line.

"Amos, are you still there?"

A grunt was all Amos could manage.

"Well, can you go?"

Amos then said the word that would begin the worst Christmas vacation of his life.

"Yes."

Chapter·2

They arrived on Christmas Eve after a long boring drive across endless flatland. There was almost nothing to do except play cards hour after hour, and Dunc won. All the time.

This gave Amos plenty of time to think. Inside one hundred miles he was certain he would be a stain in the snow. He had never skied before, and now they were going to ski at a place called the Bloody Ridge Ski Resort. The name did not inspire confidence.

They drove into the lodge area of the ski resort after dark. Dunc pointed out a sign that hung over the entrance. He always paid close attention to signs and warnings.

WELCOME TO THE FIFTH ANNUAL
SPEED SLALOM RACE

"Maybe they'll close down the steeper slopes for the race." Amos studied the sign. "And I'll live . . ."

Dunc shook his head. "See? There's a small run called the Fuzzy Bunny slope. That's where we'll start." Dunc was pointing to a gentle-looking hill with a few beginning skiers struggling down it.

But Amos wasn't looking at the Fuzzy Bunny. He was seeing a different slope. It was an evil-looking vertical white cliff. People were plummeting down at speeds that made them almost disappear.

As they walked into the lodge, Amos stopped in front of the map of the ski area.

"The names of the runs read like horror movies."

"The Mogul Mutilator, Blood Drinker, Skull Masher, Spleen Ripper, Disembow-

6

eler—yeah you're right. Sounds great." Dunc had his usual grin. "Let's get to the room. I'll write up an itinerary for us before we go to bed. That way we can maximize our slope time in the morning."

"You mean minimize my chance to survive." Amos walked upstairs.

They went to bed, but Amos couldn't sleep. He kept tossing and turning and dreaming horrible nightmares about plummeting. He hated the thought of plummeting.

In a little while the dream changed. He dreamed he was swimming peacefully in a gentle woodland pool—away from the skiing. Away from his nightmare.

Amos woke up with a start.

His head was soaking wet, and he felt as if he were trying to breathe water. He opened his eyes to find his head in the toilet.

"Amos, you could at least use the shower." Dunc stood at the bathroom door.

"I guess I was sleepwalking. Ever since that time with the monkey who stole toilets,

I've had this problem. I mean, at first I dreamed of skiing, and then it changed to . . ." He coughed up some toilet water.

"Let's get our skis and get to the slopes." Dunc was dressed and halfway out the door while Amos was still struggling with his pants.

Chapter·3

Twenty minutes later they stood at the top of the Fuzzy Bunny listening to a boring instructor with a monotone voice. He droned on and on about skiing. He made skiing sound like Mr. Trasky's history class. Amos's attention wandered.

There were people gathering by the entrance of the ski lodge far below. Many looked like reporters—no, ant reporters, with their ant cameras and ant microphones ready and waiting by the main doors to the lodge.

". . . watch out for the left side of the beginner's slope. It drops off onto the Spleen

Ripper, a slightly more advanced ski slope."
The instructor pointed toward the side of
the hill that dropped off almost vertically
toward the ski lodge.

Amos's attention snapped back at the
mention of Spleen Ripper, but he was too
late.

"What was that warning?" Amos looked
concerned.

"Oh, nothing to worry about." Dunc
stepped into his ski bindings. "This is gonna
be great." Dunc had a broad smile on his
face. His cheeks were rosy from the cold.

"Yeah, I can hardly wait." Amos was
straight-faced, looking sick and a little
green.

Amos watched Dunc start down the
slope, carefully "snowplowing" with his ski
tips aimed inward. This, so the instructor
said, gave you control. "Shift something
from one leg to the other to turn," Amos remembered the instructor saying—but he
couldn't remember what to shift.

Amos heaved a sigh and began a creep-
ing descent of the Fuzzy Bunny with a

semisuccessful snowplow. At first he attempted to follow Dunc's path. But his left ski hit a patch of ice.

The skis seemed to dart out from under him. Frantically he managed to push forward enough with the poles to help his body catch up to his legs, but that only increased his speed.

In moments he was completely out of control.

The trees screamed past. Everything became a white blur. He roared downward faster, and without knowing it he committed a fatal error.

He slipped off of the Fuzzy Bunny.

Onto the Spleen Ripper.

He felt like the chickens he had read about that they used for testing airplane windshields. They fired the chickens at aircraft canopies from giant air guns to test the effect of birds on the glass.

Amos was now an "air chicken."

All he needed was a window.

He saw camera flashes. Below him a group of people were gathered—the ant reporters who had distracted him in the first place. He was bearing down on them at the speed of light.

It was already too late. He plowed through them in a giant white explosion of skis and snow.

And then he found his window.

At something near terminal velocity he hit the huge picture window in the restaurant of the lodge.

The window only slowed him a little—it was the stuffed Kodiak bear by the fireplace that really stopped him. The bear was mounted to look ferocious, reared up on its hind legs with its teeth bared.

It was the last thing Amos saw before he lost consciousness.

Chapter · 4

"Young man, are you all right?" It was a calm voice from somewhere in space.

Amos opened his eyes to see an impossibly handsome man. He had short-trimmed dark hair. His teeth were pearly white, and he was smiling gently. There was a dimple in his chin. He looked like Superman or a game show host. The man wore the latest fashion in fluorescent ski clothes and could have been a model from a ski catalog.

"Air chicken. I'm an air chicken." Amos spat bear fur and rubbed his head. They were the last words that had gone through his mind. "Are you a ski angel?"

He looked around. He saw camera flashes sparkling everywhere around him. No, not *around* him—*at* him. For once, he was the center of attention, and the first words out of his mouth were, "I'm an air chicken."

"It seems you've been rapped on the head." The man turned to a waiter. "Get him some hot cocoa."

Dunc came walking through the broken window toward Amos, and his face instantly lit with recognition.

"You're Francesco Bartoli." Dunc stopped in his tracks staring at the man, ignoring Amos.

"Hello. Are you a friend of his?" Francesco pointed toward Amos, still sprawled in front of the stuffed bear.

"Oh . . . yeah. Amos, are you all right? I saw you pass me and fly down the Spleen Ripper."

"Window. Big window." Amos couldn't get his mouth to work.

"We better get him to his bed." Francesco pointed toward the stairway that went up to the rooms.

"Right." Dunc helped Francesco carry Amos to the room and put him on the bed.

"Are you here for the race?" Dunc asked Francesco, throwing a cover over Amos. He tucked the corners with a crisp hospital fold.

"Yes. You're here to ski, I take it?"

"Amos and I just started, but I'm a big fan of yours. You did great in the Olympics."

"Thank you. I have to get back to the press, but maybe if you and your friend are up to it, I could give you some private lessons later."

"Are you kidding? That would be excellent, wouldn't it, Amos?"

"Bear, big bear." Amos stared glassy-eyed as Francesco left. His mind came back. "Who was that?"

"I owe you again, Amos. That was Francesco Bartoli, the famous skier. I never would have met him if it wasn't for you running through his press conference."

"Don't mention it." Amos tried to get up, but the sheets were tucked so tight, he couldn't move.

"He's won five gold medals. My dad always watched him on the Winter Olympics. And now he's going to teach us how to ski. Isn't that great?"

"Gee, I can hardly wait." Amos picked the last of the bear fur from his teeth.

Chapter · 5

"Mom and I are going to the mall. Are you coming?" Dunc was putting on his jacket, lining the side seams of the jacket exactly with the side seams of his ski pants.

"Yeah, wait up." Amos had just awakened from his nap. The morning's air chicken incident had taken a lot out of him.

"I'll wait down in the car." Dunc left.

Amos was happy to be doing something besides skiing. In fact, he was happy to be doing *anything* but skiing. He put on his coat and went to the parking lot.

The rental van was sitting there, its engine idling. He could see people inside, and what appeared to be Dunc sitting behind the tinted window. It's time, Amos thought, to get a little revenge.

Amos crouched and hid in back of a trash container, sliding it along in front of him until he was next to the window. Then he took a deep breath, inflated his cheeks, smudged his face into the glass, blew as hard as he could, and made a sound like a rhino with gas.

Amos opened his eyes.

The blood drained from his face.

It wasn't Dunc.

It wasn't even a boy.

It was Melissa.

Melissa here at the Bloody Ridge Ski Resort.

She stared back at him, her eyes wide.

"Uunnnggg . . ." Amos's mind reeled. He wanted to say something witty, anything. But he couldn't. He tried again. "Thuuunngg . . ."

Frantically he looked for the right van, found it, and slithered into the seat next to Dunc.

"Amos, what's wrong? You're white."

Dunc had been picking loose threads off his ski pants.

"M-M-M-Mel—Melissa." Amos was shaking violently.

"Melissa, here?" Dunc smiled. "Now you'll *have* to ski."

"No, no more death in the snow."

"What better way to impress her than by showing off your abilities on the slopes?" Dunc nudged Amos with his elbow. "Besides, with Francesco giving us private lessons, you'll be a great skier in no time."

"After this morning you would be lucky to get me back into the state again. Let alone on the slopes." Amos's color began to return. "Do you think she saw me skiing this morning?"

"She probably wouldn't have recognized you—you were moving so fast. You also have to remember, she doesn't really know you're alive."

Amos ignored that comment. "Do you think private lessons would really help me?"

"It's a beginning." Dunc knew he had Amos now. "We'll start tomorrow."

Chapter · 6

"Are you hungry?" Dunc pointed toward a restaurant called the Gooey Spoon Eatery. "I'm starving."

"Sure, whatever." Amos was still depressed. He hadn't quit thinking about Melissa in the two hours they had been at the mall.

Amos decided to eat light and ordered only two Belly Bomber Bucket o' Burgers and a Bushel o' Fries and sat down.

"You know, Amos, those burgers are bad for you." Dunc sat down with his chef salad and carefully arranged his plastic silverware.

"What's the difference? I won't live to be eighteen if I follow you around." Amos unhinged his lower jaw and pounded down a burger.

"Hey, look." Dunc pointed toward a man wearing sunglasses and a full-length black leather coat. He was carrying a briefcase, standing by the pay phone. "He looks like he's waiting for someone."

"No, absolutely not." Amos swallowed like a wolf. "You want to investigate, and that *always* means trouble."

"Come on, Amos." Dunc folded his napkin and started to get up. "Where's your sense of adventure?"

"It's smeared somewhere over the Spleen Ripper."

"He's meeting somebody." Dunc looked at another man, who seemed exactly the same as the first one. They met and talked briefly. Then they started walking away together. "We've got to hurry."

"Oh, all right." Amos gave in. He had finished his burgers anyway. He burped. "I'm going to regret this."

Dunc and Amos left the Gooey Spoon and walked toward the men.

"They're going toward the bathrooms," Dunc pointed out. "I bet they're going to trade briefcases. Do you think they're spies?"

"Do you know what happens when you mess with spies?" Amos whined. "Think of all those James Bond movies."

"This could be the best Christmas vacation ever." Dunc walked faster. " 'Dunc Bond and his trusty sidekick, Amos Binder, 007.' "

Dunc and Amos followed the two men into the rest room. The men were talking quietly in a toilet stall.

"Psst—in here!" Dunc whispered for Amos to follow him into the adjacent stall.

They both climbed onto the toilet seat and stood, listening intently.

One of the men was speaking. "This should do it. Here's your stuff. Did you bring the cash?" He sounded as if he had eaten sandpaper for breakfast.

"Here, take your money." The other man

had a smooth voice with an English accent. "This special resin had better work."

"Hey, if it doesn't cause Bartoli to lose control after you put it on his skis, just come and find me." The raspy voice was threatening. "I'd be happy to return the money to you. But I can guarantee Bartoli will crash. It'll turn his skis to grease." He stopped talking abruptly. "Shh, somebody's coming."

The door to the bathroom opened, and several people came in laughing.

"Dunc, they sound like girls." Amos was whispering. "We aren't in the girl's bathroom, are we?"

"I didn't check. Be quiet." Dunc put his finger to his lips. The men were also silent.

". . . and then he inflated his lips on the window." It was Melissa.

"I'm so sure. What a geek!"

Another girl asked, "Did you know who it was?"

"He looked familiar, but I couldn't place him." Melissa hesitated. "Wait a sec—he was the same one who ran through Francesco's press conference. Amos something . . ."

"Uunnggg . . ." Amos's knees buckled as he stood on top of the toilet seat.

"What was that?" The other girl laughed.

"I'm not sure," Melissa answered.

Amos collapsed.

Chapter · 7

Dunc tried to grab Amos, but he was too late.

Amos's left foot caught in the toilet paper dispenser, and his right foot splashed in the toilet bowl.

"What was that?" Both the men and the girls shouted at once.

Amos sprawled out on the floor. His face went under the stall partition. The men stood there staring down at him. He looked like a deer caught in the headlights.

A dead deer.

"He's been there all the time. He heard

everything. Get him!" The man with the raspy voice lunged down for him.

"Run for it, Amos!" Dunc flew out of the stall and headed for the bathroom door. Amos struggled to his feet and followed Dunc through the stall door.

His left foot dragged toilet paper, and his right foot sloshed from the toilet water.

Melissa and her friend stared as Dunc and Amos thundered past them, chased by the two men, out the door, pounding back out into the mall.

Something caught Dunc's eye as they whipped past the toy store. "Amos—your foot," he gasped, his feet pounding.

Amos looked down. From his left foot, toilet paper was stretching back behind him, trailing from the the girls' rest room. Amos shook his foot, but the paper was stuck fast. People started to notice them.

"Hey, that's the kid from the press conference—that one who hit the bear—"

"Quick, in here!" Dunc ran into a pet store and Amos followed, leaving his toilet paper trail.

The clerk had his back to the counter

and didn't notice them. "Head for that back door," Dunc said without missing his stride.

They went through the door beneath a sign that neither of them saw. It was an important sign. It read . . .

BEWARE: DANGEROUS ANIMALS

Stacked around the room were large animal shipping containers, with solid metal sides and small cage windows in the doors. But the lights were off and it was hard to see. "It's dark in here. Where did you go, Dunc?"

"In here. Come on, I can hear them coming." Dunc slid into one of the cases and crouched down.

Amos fumbled around in the dark until he felt his way in. "Dunc, why is your breath so bad?"

Dunc's answer sounded far away. "You're not in my box."

There was a deep growl next to Amos.

Chapter · 8

Just then the door creaked open and the light from the pet shop spilled into the room.

The shadow of the two men moved across the floor.

Amos sat in suspense. "If I'm not in your box, then what's in here with me?" Amos hissed. There was another low growl.

"Shhh."

"The toilet paper leads in here." The man with the sandpaper voice was pointing to the trail that led directly to the case Amos was in.

He followed it.

Amos heard another growl, and turned to see two glowing eyes in the shadows behind him.

Red eyes.

The man now standing in front of Amos's case snorted as he bent over to open the latch. The glowing red eyes blinked.

There was an explosion of fur like a hair bomb blowing up, and the man was jerked off his feet and dragged into the cage with Amos.

"Eeeaaaah!"

"It's a wolverine cage, Bill. Says so right here on the label. You'd better get out of there."

It was too late.

Dunc watched from his container. He thought that the cage looked like those suitcases that the gorilla in the commercials tosses around.

And Amos was inside it. The cage tumbled across the floor, emitting screams and growls, and hit the wall with a thump. Somehow, some way, Amos dragged himself out. He was covered with toilet paper and had a wolverine wrapped around his leg.

"Get it off, Dunc!" Amos tried to run. But the wolverine tripped him, and the two of them flopped past the man at the door and out of the room.

Instead of chasing Amos, the man moved to help his friend, who was still inside the wolverine container, bleeding from a thousand scratches.

Dunc used the moment to make a break for it. He burst out of the cage and sprinted for the door. He followed the screams and shredded toilet paper trail until he saw a crowd.

"Ge . . . i . . . helf . . ." Dunc heard Amos's muffled cries.

"Amos, quit playing with the pets. We've gotta get out of here." Dunc moved to the center of the crowd.

"Dnc . . . helf . . ." Now the wolverine was wrapped around Amos's face like a furry wet towel. His clothes were torn to rags.

"Hold still, Amos." Dunc pulled the wolverine off Amos as if he were defusing a bomb. The wolverine tried to bite at Dunc, but he pushed it aside. It would have turned

33

back on Dunc except that it discovered a woman with a pink poodle on the end of a leash. The wolverine went for the poodle.

"The room is spinning, Dunc." Amos wobbled from side to side. "Is the monster gone? Where am I?"

"Don't open your eyes yet, Amos." Dunc steadied him. "You'll wish you hadn't."

Amos opened his eyes.

He was looking right into the face of Melissa.

For the third time that day, he fainted.

Chapter · 9

"Guess what, Amos? They're gonna let you out of here." Dunc walked through the door of Amos's hospital room,

"I just got here. They're not going to turn me loose again, are they?" Amos had hoped to spend the rest of his vacation in the safety of the hospital.

"Well, they do have some things to do with you first." Dunc sat down.

"Things? What things?" Amos was getting nervous.

"Just the shots."

"Shots?" Amos went white.

"After all, you were wearing a wolverine

on your face." Dunc shrugged. "The police haven't found out who those guys were yet."

"Shots? How big is the needle?"

"They asked me some questions." Dunc leaned forward to whisper, "But I made sure I didn't tell them about what we heard in the bathroom."

"Is it one of those square needles?"

"I figured that if I told them, we wouldn't get all the credit ourselves." Dunc arranged the magazines on the bedstand. "For a hospital they sure are sloppy. The dates on these magazines aren't even in the proper sequence."

"Credit for what, Dunc?"

"The big bust." Dunc put the magazines in chronological order. "We'll save Francesco at just the right moment."

"I don't want anything to do with it." Amos folded his arms. "You've gotten me into enough trouble already."

"Amos, think it through." Dunc looked up from the magazines. "Melissa thinks you're a geek now, right?"

"Yeah." Amos stared at Dunc.

"Well, when we save Francesco, I'll make

36

sure you get the credit." Dunc straightened the lampshade by the bed.

Amos looked unimpressed.

"Francesco is the heartthrob of every girl in school. If you save him, you'll be the envy of all of them, especially Melissa."

"But what if those men come after us?" Amos thought about the James Bond movies again. But then, James Bond always got the girl.

"Don't worry, Amos."

The doctor walked in, holding a long dripping syringe. "Amos Binder?"

It happened again. Amos fainted.

Chapter · 10

"You should eat cereal, Amos." Dunc crunched his Bran-Nuts. "Those pancakes and syrup have thousands of calories."

"I'll need all the energy I can get to follow you around." Amos wolfed down half a pancake in one bite. "Besides, that cereal looks like gravel."

"While you were still asleep, Francesco called." Dunc swallowed. "He said he would give us lessons this morning."

"Did you tell him about those men?"

"No, I thought that if we caught them on our own, it would look better." Dunc spooned up some skim milk.

"Shouldn't we tell him? Remember that they were going to do something to his skis."

"If we tell him, no one will believe we saved him." Dunc stood up. "You *do* want Melissa to think you saved him, don't you?"

They went to the Fuzzy Bunny, where they found Francesco waiting. "Good morning, boys. How are you today?"

"Great, absolutely great!" Dunc was so excited he was shaking.

Amos was shaking too.

"What's wrong, Amos?" Dunc tapped Amos's shoulder.

Amos was looking down toward the lodge. "Those two men—the spies are down there."

"Spies?" Francesco looked down the slope. "What spies?"

"Could you excuse us?" Dunc turned toward Francesco and whispered, "I don't think he's fully recovered from his crash yet."

"Hmmm. Maybe we had better wait on the lessons then. What do you think?"

Dunc nodded.

"Come find me when he's feeling better,

okay?" Francesco turned and walked back toward the chairlift.

Dunc turned back to his friend. "Did you really see them, Amos?"

"Just one."

"Did he see you?" Dunc squinted down at the lodge to see more clearly.

"I don't think so."

"Let's follow him." Dunc started down to the lodge.

"Wait—remember the last time we followed him?" Amos stood up fast. "I got to wear a roll of toilet paper, not to mention a wolverine."

"Oh, come on, Amos. That was exciting. Besides, don't forget that Melissa has a crush on Francesco."

With a sigh Amos gave in.

They walked down to the lodge where Amos had seen the man.

"Did you see where he went?" Dunc looked around like a secret service agent.

"He walked that way." Amos pointed toward the parking lot. "There he is."

"He's walking toward Francesco's van. Let's hurry."

41

"He's getting into the driver's seat." Amos had to jog to keep up with Dunc. "He's gonna steal the van."

"Quick, run for the back door!" Dunc broke into an all-out lope. "We'll find out where they're going."

"Shouldn't we report this?" Amos said, following. But it was too late.

Dunc opened the back door and threw himself into the van before Amos could say anything more. With a heave, Amos launched himself into the door too.

"Get under these ski clothes." Dunc climbed into a pile of jackets in the corner of the van.

The back of the van was filled with Francesco's ski equipment.

They lay hidden quietly listening for clues, but all they heard was the sound of the engine.

The van came to a sudden halt.

They heard the driver get out and someone talking.

Then with a click the back door opened.

Chapter · 11

"All of Francesco's skis should be in here."

"I'm sure no one saw me steal the van." The weasely man climbed in. "If we hurry, we can get it back before it's missed."

Amos was short of breath. He felt as if he were being smothered.

"Harley, sit down and hold the skis while I put this resin on."

Harley sat down on the ski clothes—and Amos's head.

Amos froze and lay there while the men worked on the skis. He could no longer breathe. At last he sucked in air with a whooshing sound.

"What the—" The man heard the noise and threw the clothes aside. "Hey! You're the one from the mall!"

He reached down and grabbed Amos by the collar.

Amos struggled to break free, but the man's grip was too strong.

"How much do you know, kid?" The man picked Amos up off the floor like a toy. "And you had better tell the truth."

"I don't know anything—I mean, know about what?" Amos had never been very good at lying under pressure. Actually, Amos wasn't very good at lying, period.

"Put him in one of those crates until the ski race is over, then it won't matter." Harley pointed over his shoulder. There was a warehouse next to where the van was parked and lots of wooden boxes.

"Yeah, no one would believe this kid anyway." Bill held Amos high enough to look straight into his eyes. "By the time the race is over, we'll be on our way out of the country."

Amos looked down at the pile of clothes

that still hid Dunc, then realized the man had followed his gaze.

"What are you looking at, kid?" Bill looked down at the clothes. "That's right. You had a friend with you, didn't you?"

"Dunc, run!" Amos struggled to get free, flopping like a caught fish.

Dunc sprang up and ran right into Harley, who said, "Gotcha."

"I'm sure these are the only two who know," Bill said. "Let's get them into the crates."

"You won't get away with this, you know," said Dunc.

"Oh, yeah? We'll see about that." Bill put Dunc in a large crate.

"We know all your plans." Dunc looked smug. "Don't we, Amos?"

"Dunc, shut up." Amos bit his lip. "Remember what I said about James Bond movies?"

"Good advice, Dunc. Shut up." Harley smiled a twisted grin. " 'Nighty-night."

With Amos and Dunc tucked into the crate, the men put the cover on and nailed it shut.

Chapter·12

"Well, Dunc, what now?" Amos listened to the van pull away. "They're getting away, and we're stuffed in a box."

"What would James Bond do?" Dunc pulled out the penlight on his key chain.

"You're not James Bond." Amos blinked from the light. "James Bond wouldn't have gotten crammed into a crate."

"I've got an idea." Dunc rubbed his chin thoughtfully. "Start feeling around for a weak spot in the crate."

"Why?"

"I'll tell you when we find one." Dunc felt the seams of the box.

After a few minutes, Dunc found what he thought was a small crack.

"All right, now take your coat off." Dunc unzipped his own jacket, managed to get it off, and set it beside Amos.

Amos looked at him suspiciously.

"Come on, Amos. We have to hurry, or they're going to get away."

"What harebrained idea do you have now?" Amos struggled to remove his ski jacket in the tight quarters. "This is going to hurt, isn't it?"

"It shouldn't be too bad Amos. We're going to use our heads to get out of this one."

"I had figured on using my brain, Dunc, but what are we going to do?"

"That's not what I meant." Dunc tapped his forehead. "I meant we are going to use our *heads*."

"You're not serious. You want me to ram the box open with my head?"

"Use the sleeves to tie the jackets around your ears."

"Aren't you going to do this too?" Amos pointed the penlight at Dunc's ski jacket lying beside him.

"No, we're going to need all the padding for one head." Dunc studied the crack. "Besides, one of us has to hold the light."

"Why do I let you do this to me?" Amos started tying on his improvised crash helmet.

"Your folds are sloppy, but that looks about right." Dunc studied Amos's helmet with the penlight when he had finished. "Can you see out of that?"

"Barely."

"It makes you look like one of those cartoon characters with the huge heads." Dunc laughed.

"Shut up."

"All right, let's get started. And try not to get us covered with wood chips."

Amos lined up just right, pulled back with his neck, and let fly.

Whuunnk!

His head stopped cold.

It sounded like a melon thumped to be tested for ripeness.

"A little to the left." Dunc checked the seam with his fingers. "You missed."

"Ohhh . . ." Amos gave a muffled moan.

Whuunnk!

"Ohhh . . ." Amos's right leg spasmed.

"Now to the right, just a hair." Dunc resumed the role of foreman.

Crack!

The box splintered open along the seam. Dim sunlight streamed through the hole.

"Good work, Amos." Dunc started removing splinters from his hair. "A little messy, though."

"Ohh . . ."

"Let's get after them."

"Ohh . . ."

Chapter · 13

"Ge dis ting off a me." Amos struggled with the bundle of jackets tied around his head.

"Hold still." Dunc worked at the knots, but they wouldn't come undone. "I can't get it, and we have to get going."

"I not gone anywha wi dis on my hed."

"You can still breathe, right?"

"Ya."

"You can see, right?"

"Ya. Sorba, a liddle bid."

"Then what are you worried about? Let's go." Dunc went out the warehouse door and into the street before Amos could say anything.

"There's a bus stop." Dunc pointed to the sign. "Let's try to get on to a bus."

A large blue commuter bus pulled up just then, and Dunc dragged Amos to the door.

The driver looked down at them.

"Where y'all headed, boys?" It was an old man with small round glasses and a blue uniform.

"To the Bloody Ridge Ski Resort." Dunc pulled Amos up the stairs of the bus. "We have to save Francesco."

"Who's that, your dog?" The driver looked at Amos oddly. "Oh, it's a kid. Say kid, do you know you have jackets tied on yer head? That ain't gonna do much fer the cold."

"Gee, danks." Amos hit his head on the doorframe but didn't seem to notice.

"Well, you boys ain't going nowhere, less'n ya give me some money." The old man held out his hand.

"Money, Amos. I left mine in the room."

"Id's in ma coad pocked." Amos fumbled with the pocket zipper on his forehead. "I can't get id. Id's on da inside."

"Gee, I'm sorry, sir, but we can't seem to get our money." Dunc put on his best begging face. "Could you please give us a ride to the ski resort? Our parents will pay."

"Why is it you need to get there so awfully bad?" The driver had no other passengers, and seemed interested in what the boys were up to.

"We're going to save Francesco Bartoli." Dunc sighed. "Someone is trying to sabotage his skis so he'll lose the race."

"*The* Francesco Bartoli? The world-famous skier?" The man's eyes sparkled. "You ain't kidd'n me, are ya, boy?"

"Would I kid you?"

"Well, why didn't ya say somth'n earlier?" He threw his thumb over his shoulder. "Get in and sit down. This is gonna be the ride of yer life!"

He laughed gleefully and drove the gas pedal through the floor.

Chapter · 14

The driver threw his uniform cap over his shoulder and reached under the seat.

"Heck, I haven't had a chance to drive like this since my accident." He pulled out a weather-beaten cowboy hat that said "Tex" on the front and plopped it on his head. "I'm gonna love this."

He dug into his uniform pocket and pulled out a pair of black leather driving gloves—the kind of gloves high-performance race car drivers wear.

"Sir, we nod im dad big a rush." Amos's muffled plea came like a whimper. "Ya cod slow dowd a bid."

They screamed past another bus stop. Four people waiting had to dive for safety.

"What you say'n, boy?" The man looked in his mirror at Amos. "I can't hear ya with all that stuff on yer head."

"Look ad da road." Amos pointed at an oncoming trash truck.

"Ah, that ain't noth'n. I used to ride bulls in the rodeo." With a flick of his wrist, Tex the Bus Driver pulled the bus up onto the sidewalk.

"This is just like the movies, huh, Amos?" Dunc stood up in the front of the bus, looking out. "Like a James Bond movie."

"Dell me wen id's ober." Amos crawled onto the floor between the seats and put his hands over his padded head.

"I hear sirens." Dunc glanced out the back of the bus and then at Tex.

"Never met a smokey yet who could catch me." Tex looked into his mirror. "They always used to chase me when I ran moonshine back in the thirties."

The bus careened down the sidewalk.

"Hold on, boys." He threw the steering

wheel hard to the left, and the tail end of the bus screeched around, leveling a lamp-post and a phone booth.

"Whhaaahoooo!" Tex looked at Dunc. "I call that move a Bootlegger. Dates back to my smuggling days."

Three police cars, lights flashing, came barreling down the street straight at the bus.

"Watch this, boys!" Tex slammed his foot to the floor, and the bus's tires screamed. He yelled out the window. "Give it up! Yer mess'n with Elmer Peasley, meanest bus driver north of the Rio Grande!"

The bus lurched and roared forward directly at the squad cars.

At the last minute, the police cars swerved to miss the bus and blew through the walls of the surrounding buildings.

"Got rid of *them*." Tex smiled. "Ain't had this much fun in a long time."

"Uh . . . great. Could you please get us to the ski resort now?" Dunc realized he'd been holding his breath all the time, and now he took a lungful.

"Ya got it, sonny."

The bus tore down the street and out of town toward the ski resort.

"There's the van, Amos." Dunc pointed to it as they approached the ski resort parking lot. "We've made it. The race hasn't started yet."

He was right. They would have made it with plenty of time to spare, with no problems.

Except that Tex didn't see the stock truck full of sheep.

Chapter · 15

The bus had to be going at least seventy when it hit the sheep truck.

There was a scrunch like a giant aluminum can being crushed and the sound of sheep baying. Both the bus and the stock truck came to a halt.

"Whad happid?" Amos's padded head was jammed under the seat.

"You don't want to know." Dunc looked around him.

There were sheep everywhere—climbing all over the inside of the bus.

"I hates sheeps." Tex stood up, brushed off his cowboy hat, and heaved a ewe off his lap. "They smell like sewers, and they flat mess *up* a bus. You boys all right?"

"Fine, thanks for the ride." Dunc pushed a sheep aside and dragged Amos out from under the seat. "Come on, Amos, we're there."

A sheep nuzzled Amos in the face, licking him through the folds of his helmet.

"Duc, is dad a seep? I hear seep."

"Yeah, and it looks like he likes you." Dunc helped Amos to his feet. "Quit messing with him. We don't have much time."

They leaped from the back door of the bus and ran toward the van.

The sheep, which was so fat that it looked like a ball of wool, followed Amos closely.

Amos let a loud sneeze go, one that should have knocked him over. "Duc, is dad seep wid us? I'm allergic do wool."

"Yeah. I'll get rid of him." Dunc stopped and flailed his hands at the sheep to scare him off. "He won't go, he likes you. We'll just have to outrun him."

They ran to the parking lot.

"There's no one in the van. Let's check the back." Dunc opened the back door.

"Rats! Its empty!" Dunc looked in at the vacant ski racks. "That means Francesco has already picked up his skis for the race."

A loudspeaker blared from the slopes:

"Ladies and gentlemen, our first racer, John Lewiston, will now make his run, followed by Francesco Bartoli."

"Quick, put this on!" Dunc grabbed two Team Bartoli ski jackets. "These will get us past security, into the race area."

"I dond know uf we shodd dake dese. Iddn't it stealing?"

"We don't have time to worry about that—let's move." Dunc thrust the jacket at Amos.

They ran toward the chair lift, the sheep following. Dunc looked up to where Francesco would race—it was the meanest slope, the Disemboweler.

Amos stopped dead.

Chapter · 16

"I can't do da chair lif."

A chair passed the boarding point.

"It can't be that difficult." Dunc reached out for Amos's arm. "We just have to step up to the line and sit down at the right moment."

"Whud if we fall off? Id's a long way dowd."

Another chair passed.

"Come on, Amos." Dunc pulled Amos to the loading position.

Almost.

As the chair came swinging around, Dunc sat down with ease, but it caught

Amos high in the back and toppled him over.

"Duc, I'm gonna—*ummff.*"

As he fell, his jacket caught the arm of the seat and held and dragged him up.

And up.

"Duc, I'm gonna—" Amos looked down. "Wahhh!"

"Hold on, Amos!" From the chair Dunc tried to grab for Amos, but he couldn't. "I can't reach you. I'll fall if I do."

"Dat wouldn't be zo bad." Amos was mad.

He hung there, over a hundred feet in the air, like a mouse dangling in a hawk's talons.

"Hey, look at that TV!" Dunc pointed toward an enormous video monitor that stood over a large crowd. "That's the biggest screen I've ever seen."

"Imagine how mush ah care." Amos tried to find a grip without looking down.

"That must be the ski race." Dunc looked down over the crowd. "Amos, check the screen. Look at what's on!"

Amos twisted around.

64

There in Technicolor was Amos being an air chicken, blowing a hole in the window and flying into the stuffed bear.

Then it showed Francesco helping him up, and the crowd cheered.

"It looks like Francesco got some good publicity from your stunt, Amos."

"Gread, I'm zo glad I could hep him oud." Amos looked up at Dunc. "Ya now sumding? For all dis trubble, Melizza bedder marry me."

"Amos, heads up!" Dunc pointed toward the oncoming ramp.

Amos ignored Dunc's warning. "Ya don'd eben care aboud whad happeds do me do ya? I mean, I dink ya like do zee me ged in trubble all the ti—"

He hit the exit ramp—headfirst.

His "helmet" saved him from any permanent injury, but when he hit, he skipped and dragged. Snow embedded itself in his clothing before his jacket ripped and he fell free. He tried to drag himself up from the snow.

"D-D-Duc, c-c-cold." Amos tore at his clothes. "Godda ged dis off."

"Leave it. There they are." Dunc pointed to the two men, dressed to look like skiers, standing in the crowd. "Let's get 'em."

"Duc, l-l-listen." Amos stopped.

The speaker echoed again. *"And in two minutes, Francesco Bartoli, the defending champion, will attempt to set a new record as the world champion slalom speed racer."*

"We've got to get his skis before he races." Dunc looked at the men. "You go for the skis—I'll go get the police and bust the men."

Dunc pushed Amos toward the starting chutes before he could argue and ran off toward the men.

"B-b-but . . ." Amos let it trail off and bumbled for the gates.

"One minute to Bartoli's run," the intercom called again.

Amos looked behind him for Dunc, but he saw only the man with the sandpaper voice, running straight toward the platform as fast as he could, glaring at him.

"Five."

"F-F-Frandesco, are ya up dere?" Amos ran up the stairs and into the chute.

66

"What is it?" Francesco's voice came from behind the door. He had taken his skis off to check the bindings and was about to put them back on.

"Four."

Amos opened the door. "You can'd race. Dey mezzed wid yer skeez."

"Three."

"I can't understand what you're saying, with all that stuff on your head." He had his helmet and goggles on and was just about to step into the ski bindings.

"Two."

"No, don'd." Amos desparately grabbed at the skis.

"One."

Amos then did something he would question for the rest of his days. He stepped into the bindings. Whatever his reasoning, he had committed himself.

"Go!"

Then the world fell away.

And Amos fell with it.

On the Disemboweler.

Chapter · 17

It took a fraction of a second for Amos to realize what had happened.

The Disemboweler.

The most professional ski run in the world, and he was on it after only three hours of skiing.

The slope dropped vertically, and he screamed down it, somehow staying up— barely staying alive.

He came to a bend in the run and tried to snowplow to slow down.

He shouldn't have.

As he brought his feet together, Bartoli's finely sharpened edges dug into the slope and his skis somehow crossed. He didn't fall. Instead, he seemed to pick up speed. I am on sticks of death, he thought, with my legs tangled.

On the Disemboweler.

The world seemed a blur to Amos. He managed a backward glance through the slit in his jacket helmet.

There was nobody there.

He was all alone.

He looked forward again just in time to catch the first slalom flagpole across the face. The helmet padded it enough, but the flag went with him, dragging behind like a streamer.

He hit the next one and took it with him too.

Soon he had three, then four of the flags hanging off of him, trailing out behind him.

The dragging flags slowed him somewhat, but another bend was rocketing toward him. He managed a quick cross-legged turn—not bad, considering he was doing over sixty miles an hour—and with much relief glided onto what seemed to be a gentler slope.

He looked again and couldn't believe his eyes. It seemed like he was coming to the edge of the earth. Just ahead, everything dropped into nothing. Then he remembered the brochure he'd read about the race. It wasn't just a slalom—they had added something.

The jump.

The last stage of the race.

As his body hurtled toward the edge of the jump, Amos mentally flashed on whose skis he was wearing—Francesco's.

He had forgotten all about the resin intended to destroy Francesco's control. At the high speed of the drop into the jump, more heat was generated and the resin finally kicked in.

As he hit the jump itself, what little control he had disappeared. His legs spread apart as the resin turned his skis to grease, and he rocketed up the jump sideways and spun like a pinwheel into space.

He flew up over the crowd in a graceless

arc that carried him into the pine trees lining the course, where he hit a tall pine. The tree gave when he hit, bent toward the ground, and set him down gently—almost.

With a wooden groan, the tree righted itself and catapulted Amos back above the crowd straight at the ski lodge. Dunc would swear later that he had left a smoke trail through the air. The wind screaming past Amos's head moved the jacket away from his eyes enough for him to see that he was aimed at the picture window.

Again.

They had worked all night repairing it, and the new glass shone brightly in the sunlight.

Amos arrowed in directly in front of the lodge, bounced once, leaving a steaming crater, and blew through the window. He somehow managed to stay on his skis until he hit the bear.

Again.

But they hadn't rebolted the bear to the floor, and this time it didn't slow him down much. Both Amos and the bear went flying out of the lodge through the window on the other side.

The window shattered in a cloud of glass. Amos and the bear plowed into the parking lot. The landing would have been more painful if he hadn't landed on the bear.

Amos lay there stunned in the snow on top of the bear. Smoke or steam rose from his clothing. His legs were still crossed, and where his jacket-helmet was torn, there was stuffing hanging out. He tried to stand, but he was tangled in the slalom flags and crossed skis and nothing seemed to work right.

He rose finally to his knees, raised one hand, and pushed the jacket-helmet up off his eyes.

He was looking right into the wide eyes of Melissa.

Then, once more, he fainted dead away.

Chapter · 18

"Hold still, it looks like the doctor missed a few splinters." Dunc used tweezers to pick something out of Amos's forehead.

They had made it back home and were watching TV in Dunc's room. Amos's face had swollen shut from a reaction to the bear fur embedded in his nostrils—he had received another shot for that. He still had problems sitting down because of it.

"I can't believe how big a fool I was." Amos had been dwelling on it ever since they left the ski resort. "Even my family saw all the stunts I pulled on national TV."

"Well, I promised that you would be more

popular." Dunc plucked another sliver. "Besides, the police did catch Bill and Harley."

"You don't think Melissa will recognize me, do you?" He ignored Dunc's optimism.

"You don't have to worry about that. She was too busy laughing to recognize anybody." Dunc arranged the slivers in a neat pile on the end table. "Twenty-seven."

"What?"

"Twenty-seven slivers. That's how many the doctor missed." He threw them in the trash can. "You did set a speed record. You even beat Bartoli's. You just gave the race officials the wrong name."

"That's because I couldn't remember my name. Now Melissa is never gonna know I was the one." Amos rolled over on his side. "I saved Francesco, and she'll never know."

"If it's any consolation, my parents have already decided to go back next year." Dunc smiled at Amos. "You know you're always welcome to come along."

Dunc almost, but didn't quite make the door before Amos hit him with a tennis shoe.

Be sure to join Dunc and Amos in these other Culpepper Adventures:

The Case of the Dirty Bird

When Dunc Culpepper and his best friend, Amos, first see the parrot in a pet store, they're not impressed—it's smelly, scruffy, and missing half its feathers. They're only slightly impressed when they learn that the parrot speaks four languages, has outlived ten of its owners, and is probably 150 years old. But when the bird starts mouthing off about buried treasure, Dunc and Amos get pretty excited—let the amateur sleuthing begin!

Dunc's Doll

Dunc and his accident-prone friend Amos are up to their old sleuthing habits once again. This time they're after a band of doll thieves! When a doll that once belonged to Charles Dickens's daughter is stolen from an exhibition at the local mall, the two boys put on their detective gear and do some serious snooping. Will a vicious watchdog keep them from retrieving the valuable missing doll?

Culpepper's Cannon

Dunc and Amos are researching the Civil War cannon that stands in the town square when they find a note inside telling them about a time portal. Entering it through the dressing room of La Petite, a women's clothing store, the boys find themselves in downtown Chatham on March 8, 1862—the day before the historic clash between the *Monitor* and the *Merrimac*. But the Confederate soldiers they meet mistake them for Yankee spies. Will they make it back to the future in one piece?

Dunc Gets Tweaked

Dunc and Amos meet up with a new buddy named Lash when they enter the radical world of skateboard competition. When somebody "cops"—steals—Lash's prototype skateboard, the boys are determined to get it back. After all, Lash is about to shoot for a totally rad world's record! Along the way they learn a major lesson: *Never* kiss a monkey!

Dunc's Halloween

Dunc and Amos are planning the best route to get the most candy on Halloween. But their plans change when Amos is slightly bitten by a werewolf. He begins scratching himself and chasing UPS trucks—he's become a werepuppy!

Dunc Breaks the Record

Dunc and Amos have a small problem when they try hang gliding—they crash in the wilderness. Luckily, Amos has read a book about a boy who survived in the wilderness for fifty-four days. Too bad Amos doesn't have a hatchet. Things go from bad to worse when a wild man holds the boys captive. Can anything save them now?

Dunc and the Flaming Ghost

Dunc's not afraid of ghosts, although Amos is sure that the old Rambridge house is haunted by the ghost of Blackbeard the Pirate. Then the best friends meet Eddie, a meek man who claims to be impersonating Blackbeard's ghost in order to live in the house in peace. But if that's true, why are flames shooting from his mouth?

Amos Gets Famous

Deciphering a code they find in a library book, Amos and Dunc stumble onto a burglary ring. The burglars' next target is the home of Melissa, the girl of Amos's dreams (who doesn't even know that he's alive). Amos longs to be a hero to Melissa, so nothing will stop him from solving this case—not even a mind-boggling collision with a jock, a chimpanzee, and a toilet.

Dunc and Amos Hit the Big Top

In order to impress Melissa, Amos decides to perform on the trapeze at the visiting circus. Look out below! But before Dunc can talk him out of his plan, the two stumble across a mystery behind the scenes at the circus. Now Amos is in double trouble. What's really going on under the big top?

Dunc's Dump

Camouflaged as piles of rotting trash, Dunc and Amos are sneaking around the town dump. Dunc wants to find out who is polluting the garbage at the dump with hazardous and toxic waste. Amos just wants to impress Melissa. Can either of them succeed?

Dunc and the Scam Artists

Dunc and Amos are at it again. Some older residents of their town have been bilked by con artists, and the two boys want to look into these crimes. They meet elderly Betsy Dell, whose nasty nephew Frank gives the boys the creeps. Then they notice some soft dirt in Ms. Dell's shed, and a shovel. Does Frank have something horrible in store for Dunc and Amos?

Dunc and Amos and the Red Tattoos

Dunc and Amos head for camp and face two weeks of fresh air—along with regulations, demerits, KP, and inedible food. But where these two best friends go, trouble follows. They overhear a threat against the camp director, and discover that camp funds have been stolen. Do these crimes have anything to do with the tattoo of the exotic red flower that some of the camp staff have on their arms?

Dunc's Undercover Christmas

It's Christmastime! and Dunc, Amos, and Amos's cousin T.J. hit the mall for some serious shopping. But when the seasonal magic is threatened by some disappearing presents, and Santa Claus himself is a prime suspect, the boys put their celebration on hold and go under-cover in perfect Christmas disguises! Can the sleuthing trio protect Santa's threatened repu-tation and catch the impostor before he strikes again?

The Wild Culpepper Cruise

When Amos wins a "Why I Love My Dog" con-test, he and Dunc are off on the Caribbean cruise of their dreams! But there's something downright fishy about Amos's suitcase, and be-fore they know it, the two best friends wind up with more high-seas adventure than they bar-gained for. Can Dunc and Amos figure out who's out to get them and salvage what's left of their vacation?

Dunc and the Haunted Castle

When Dunc and Amos are invited to spend a week in Scotland, Dunc can already hear the bagpipes a-blowin'. But when the boys spend their first night in an ancient castle, it isn't bagpipes they hear. It's moans! Dunc hears groaning coming from inside his bedroom walls. Amos notices the eyes of a painting follow him across the room! Could the castle really be haunted? Local legend has it that the castle's former lord wanders the ramparts at night in search of his head! Team up with Dunc and Amos as they go ghostbusting in the Scottish Highlands!

Cowpokes and Desperadoes

Git along, little dogies! Dunc and Amos are bound for Uncle Woody Culpepper's Santa Fe cattle ranch for a week of fun. But when they overhear a couple of cowpokes plotting to do Uncle Woody in, the two sleuths are back on the trail of some serious action! Who's been making off with all the prize cattle? Can Dunc and Amos stop the rustlers in time to save the ranch?

Prince Amos

When their fifth-grade class spends a weekend interning at the state capital, Dunc and Amos find themselves face-to-face with Amos's walking double—Prince Gustav, Crown Prince of Moldavia! His Royal Highness is desperate to uncover a traitor in his ranks. And when he asks Amos to switch places with him, Dunc holds his breath to see what will happen next. Can Amos pull off the impersonation of a lifetime?

Coach Amos

Amos and Dunc have their hands full when their school principal asks *them* to coach a local T-ball team. For one thing, nobody on the team even knows first base from left field, and the season opener is coming right up. And then there's that sinister-looking gangster driving by in his long black limo and making threats. Can Dunc and Amos fend off screaming tots, nervous mothers, and the mob, and be there when the ump yells, "Play ball"?

Amos and the Alien

When Amos and his best friend Dunc have a close encounter with an extraterrestrial named Girrk, Dunc thinks they should report their findings to NASA. But Amos has other plans. He not only promises to help Girrk find a way back to his planet, he invites him to hide out under his bed! Then weird things start to happen—Scruff can't move, Amos scores a game-winning *touchdown,* and Dunc knows Girrk is behind Amos's new powers. What's the mysterious alien really up to?

Dunc and Amos Meet the Slasher

Why is mild-mannered Amos dressed in leather, with slicked-back hair, strutting around the cafeteria and going by a phony name? Could it be because of that new kid, Slasher, who's promised to eat Amos for his lunch? Or has Amos secretly gone undercover? Amos and his pal Dunc have some hot leads and are close to cracking a stolen stereo racket, but Dunc is worried Amos has taken things too far!

For laugh-out-loud fun, join Dunc and Amos and take the Culpepper challenge!
Gary Paulsen's Culpepper Adventures—
Bet you can't read just one!

- ☐ 0-440-40790-7 DUNC AND AMOS AND THE RED TATTOOS.....$3.25/$3.99 Can.
- ☐ 0-440-40874-1 DUNC'S UNDERCOVER CHRISTMAS...............$3.50/$4.50 Can.
- ☐ 0-440-40883-0 THE WILD CULPEPPER CRUISE......................$3.50/$4.50 Can.
- ☐ 0-440-40893-8 DUNC AND THE HAUNTED CASTLE.................$3.50/$4.50 Can.
- ☐ 0-440-40902-0 COWPOKES AND DESPERADOES...................$3.50/$4.50 Can.
- ☐ 0-440-40928-4 PRINCE AMOS...$3.50/$4.50 Can.
- ☐ 0-440-40930-6 COACH AMOS...$3.50/$4.50 Can.
- ☐ 0-440-40990-X AMOS AND THE ALIENS.................................$3.50/$4.50 Can.

Bantam Doubleday Dell
Books for Young Readers

Bantam Doubleday Dell Books for Young Readers
2451 South Wolf Road
Des Plaines, IL 60018

Please send the items I have checked above. I'm enclosing $_____ (please add $2.50 to cover postage and handling). Send check or money order, no cash or C.O.D.s please.

_____
Name

_____
Address

_____
City   State   Zip

Please allow four to six weeks for delivery.
Prices and availability subject to change without notice.   BFYR 29 6/94